HOME
SAFE
HOME

BY JAKE MADDOX

text by
Brandon Terrell

NO LONGER PROPERTY OF
SEATTLE PUBLIC LIBRARY
Capitol Hill Library
JUN 26 2018

STONE ARCH BOOKS
a capstone imprint

D0018958

Jake Maddox JV Boys books are published by
Stone Arch Books
a Capstone imprint
1710 Roe Crest Drive
North Mankato, Minnesota 56003

www.mycapstone.com

Copyright © 2018 Stone Arch Books

All rights reserved. No part of this publication may be reproduced in whole or in part, or stored in a retrieval system, or transmitted in any form or by any means, electronic, mechanical, photocopying, recording, or otherwise, without written permission of the publisher.

Cataloging-in-Publication Data is available on the Library of Congress website.
ISBN: 978-1-4965-5931-9 (library binding)
ISBN: 978-1-4965-5933-3 (paperback)
ISBN: 978-1-4965-5935-7 (eBook PDF)

Summary: When Caleb's family agrees to host a college-aged ballplayer from the Dominican Republic for the summer while he plays on a local independent team, Caleb begins to rediscover the fun side of the game.

Designer: Lori Bye
Editor: Nate LeBoutillier

Photo Credits: Shutterstock: Evgenii Matrosov, chapter openers (design element), Lan V. Erickson, back cover, 1, 4, 95 (background), sirtravelalot, cover

Printed and bound in Canada.
010806S18

TABLE OF CONTENTS

CHAPTER I

THE NEW ARRIVAL

"Now arriving at gate seventeen," the voice over the airport loudspeaker said, "Flight 129 from Santo Domingo, Dominican Republic."

Fourteen-year-old Caleb Parker's ears perked up when he heard this information. "He's here!" Caleb said. "He's finally here."

Caleb's mom smiled. "Be patient," she said. "It's still going to be a few minutes."

Caleb, his mom, and his five-year-old sister, Bethany, stood in the bustling baggage claim area.

The Minneapolis-St. Paul International Airport was a flurry of activity. Men and women wearing business suits rolled compact luggage with a purpose. Families hauling more suitcases than they needed plodded past.

Caleb tapped his foot and flipped the cardboard sign in his hands over and over. On the sign was a name written in thick black marker: *Ricky Alvarez*. Caleb had written the name himself the night before.

Ricardo "Ricky" Alvarez had just been signed to play summer ball for Caleb's hometown team, the Prairie Lake Otters. The Otters were part of a small group of teams called the Northern League. Their players were usually college-age and on break from their college or club teams. Most were from the U.S., but some came from other countries. Caleb's mom had signed their family up as a host family. That meant one of the Otter players would be living with them for the summer.

When Caleb found out that their family would be hosting Ricky Alvarez, the newest member of the Otter team, he'd nearly fainted. Caleb had read about Ricky on the Internet. The shortstop had a sticky glove in the field and had hit above .300 his entire career.

"Here they come!" Caleb said. He pointed to a stream of people walking down a nearby set of stairs. Still more rode down the adjacent escalator.

"Zoom! Whoosh!" Bethany ran in circles around Caleb, her arms out like an airplane. "Coming in for a landing!"

"Knock it off," Caleb said, swatting his sign at Bethany as she buzzed around him. He craned his neck, searching the crowd for Ricky.

Through the sea of gray and black suits, Caleb spied a shock of color that made his heartbeat race. A young man in a loud Hawaiian-style shirt, an Otters baseball cap, and a pair of sunglasses leaned against the side of the descending escalator.

He looked cool and confident, unlike Caleb in pretty much every way.

"I see him," Caleb said.

"It's hard *not* to," his mom added, chuckling.

Ricky reached the bottom of the escalator. His attention turned to a young woman next to him. They chatted together and laughed. Caleb stood on his tiptoes, holding up the sign in front of him. His hands shook. The sign wobbled a bit.

Ricky and the young lady parted ways, and the celebrated ballplayer began to head in their direction. Caleb found himself getting more and more nervous with each step Ricky took.

When Ricky saw the sign in Caleb's hands, the ballplayer's already wide smile spread the length of his face. "*Hola*!" he said, his voice cutting through the crowd noise. He hurried up his pace to join the trio waiting for him.

"Hi, Ricky," Caleb said, his voice as shaky as his hands.

Ricky held out a large, callused hand, and Caleb shook it. "Pleasure to meet you," Ricky said. He spoke with an accent. "You must be Caleb."

Caleb nodded.

"Mrs. Parker." Ricky shook Caleb's mom's hand as well. "Many thanks to you for opening up your home to me this summer. I greatly appreciate it."

"You're very welcome," Caleb's mom said. "We're all excited. It'll be nice for Caleb to have someone living in the house that he can play catch with this summer."

"And one with a loco curveball," Ricky joked.

Upon hearing his mom's words about someone to play catch with, Caleb's thoughts drifted to his father. He thought about the video chats they had only once a week, if that. He thought about his dad's job on the West Coast building houses for the rich and famous. And he thought hard about his dad's new family.

"Everything okay, Caleb?" his mom asked.

Caleb shook off the sad thoughts. He didn't want them ruining this amazing new experience. "I'm good," he said.

Behind them, one of the luggage carousels beeped and began to turn. Before long, Ricky's luggage — a bright red duffel bag containing baseball gear that stood out as much as its owner did — slid down the ramp and onto the carousel.

"I got it!" said Caleb. He slipped through the waiting crowd and pulled Ricky's bag free of the moving conveyor belt. It was heavier than it looked, but he shouldered it anyway without a complaint. They headed together through the airport's glass doors.

* * *

The ride north to Prairie Lake was an hour long and mostly on a two-lane highway. The day was bright and sunny, and the temperature was already creeping into the eighties, even though it was still morning. As they drove, Ricky shared stories about his life. He talked about the Dominican Republic and how he was going to college in the fall. Caleb leaned forward in the backseat, fascinated.

When they peeled off the highway to head toward Prairie Lake, Caleb lowered his window. He let the warm summer breeze hit his face.

"Would you like to drive past the ball field?" Caleb's mom asked.

"Absolutely," Ricky said with enthusiasm.

Gordon's Hardware Field — named after the baseball diamond's sponsor — sat in the middle of town like a beating heart. All roads, like the veins of a human body, led straight to it. Caleb's mom pulled into the empty parking lot. The stadium was quite large with a covered grandstand for fans. The field's grass was a beautiful green, and an electronic scoreboard soared over the padded right field wall.

Ricky said, "This is it?"

Taken the wrong way, Ricky's words would have been an insult. Caleb's hopes for a fun and educational summer of baseball would have been dashed. But the newest Otters player's words were said with awe, like he couldn't believe what he was seeing.

Ricky turned to Caleb. "Do you have your glove?" he asked.

Caleb nodded. "It's in the trunk," he said.

"Then what are we waiting for?" asked Ricky. "Let's go!"

Ricky flung open the car door, and the two players retrieved their gloves and a battered ball from the trunk. Then they ran to the field, hopping over a short chain link fence. Caleb felt like he was breaking some sort of rule. But he was with an Otter player. No one would kick them out.

"Catch!" said Ricky. Standing near the pitcher's mound, he fired the ball to Caleb.

The ball snapped into Caleb's mitt and stung his hand.

Caleb threw the ball back to Ricky, who snagged it easily. Caleb couldn't believe it. He was standing on Gordon Field playing catch with a Prairie Lake Otter.

"Better get used to this," Ricky said, as if reading Caleb's mind. "You're about to have one memorable summer, amigo!"

CHAPTER 2

BATTING AVERAGE OR AVERAGE BATTING

One out.

One on.

One run down.

One last chance.

Caleb grabbed a bat from the rack hanging in the dugout, slid his helmet on, and stepped into the on-deck circle. Caleb's team, the East Prairie Lake Wolves, was playing its first game of the summer against the Jacksonville Lions. The Lions were one of the best teams in the league, and they'd jumped on the Wolves' pitching to get out to an 8-2 lead.

But the Wolves had fought back. It was the bottom of the seventh inning, which was the final inning at this level. Travis Weston, the Wolves' left fielder and the game's tying run, was now on second base.

If Travis didn't cross home plate, the game was over.

Eric Martinson, Caleb's best friend and the Wolves catcher, stepped up to the plate. The Lions pitcher uncorked a fastball. Eric swung and missed.

"Strike one!" the umpire bellowed.

Caleb heard a whispered round of chatter behind him in the dugout. He thought it was about Eric or possibly the Lions rock-solid reliever. But when he turned to glance back, he spied some of the players whispering and pointing to the stands.

Caleb followed their gaze. Sitting up at the top of the metal bleachers was Ricky Alvarez.

Oh man, Caleb thought. *I didn't know he was actually coming to the game.*

When Ricky saw Caleb looking in his direction, he smiled and waved. He was still wearing his Otters jersey and cap and must have come straight to the game from his own practice.

"Ball!" the ump shouted, turning Caleb's attention back to the game.

From the moment Caleb had arrived at the ball field that afternoon, his teammates had bombarded him with questions about Ricky. "What's he like?" "How fast can he throw the ball?" "Is he gonna come to any of our games?" Coach Bullock had shooed the boys away with his cap like they were a swarm of gnats. "Leave him be!" he'd shouted. "Get focused, and get out on the field!"

Caleb had never appreciated Coach Bullock's strict, no-nonsense attitude more than he had in that moment.

Eric swung at a high fastball and cracked a foul off the backstop.

"Come on," Caleb whispered under his breath. "Please don't get out."

If Eric could hit a single and score Travis from second, the pressure would be off. Caleb hated the spotlight and hated being put in any tough situations. He was definitely a vanilla ice cream-eating, no extreme sports-playing, follow-the-rules kind of kid.

In other words, he liked to play it safe.

Eric connected with the ball and hit a rocket to the right side of the infield. For a brief moment, it looked like the ball would sneak into right field and that Caleb's prayer would be answered. But the second baseman made a diving snag, popped up onto his knees, and fired a bullet to first.

"Out!" The ump jerked his thumb up.

Travis had alertly advanced to third. The tying run was now only 90 feet away.

And the outcome was all down to Caleb.

"All right, Parker!" said Coach Bullock. He spit a string of sunflower seeds out like his mouth was some kind of machine gun. "Keep your eye on the ball and take smart swings."

Caleb nodded at the coach. But he was thinking of his own strategy. *Maybe I won't swing at all. I'll try to walk. Yeah, that's a solid plan. Make the pitcher throw to me.*

The bat shook in his hands. He gripped it tighter, hoping the pitcher couldn't see how nervous he was.

A lilting whistle carried from the bleachers, cutting through the claps and cheers of the crowd. Caleb looked back to find the source of the unique sound. It was Ricky, who unleashed a second whistle that drew the attention of many parents in the stands.

"You can do it!" Ricky shouted.

Caleb stepped into the batter's box.

The first pitch sizzled past him.

Caleb didn't try to swing, hoping the pitch would be a ball.

"Strike one!"

Caleb looked down to third. Travis danced off the base, itching to score.

Caleb was sticking with his game plan, though. He knew that Anthony Carbini, a solid batter, was waiting in the on-deck circle.

If Caleb got on base, Anthony would tie it up for sure.

"Strike two!"

Caleb hadn't even noticed the pitcher in his wind-up.

"Come on, Caleb!" shouted Ricky. His whistle sliced through the air again.

The count was 0-2. The chances of walking now were tiny. Caleb was forced to abandon his plan. If the Wolves were going to send the game to extra innings, he would have to be the one to do it.

Caleb crouched and squinted at the mound.

The pitcher rocked back and went into his wind-up and hurled the ball . . .

. . . right into the dirt in front of the plate.

Before he could stop himself, Caleb swung as hard as he could. A puff of dirt exploded up as the ball bounced over the plate, hitting the catcher in the chest protector. It was an ugly pitch, and an even uglier swing.

Before Caleb could run, the Lions catcher tagged Caleb with the ball in his mitt.

"Batter's out!" called the ump.

Caleb's shoulders sunk. He watched the catcher rush off to join in on the Lions' noisy victory celebration.

The dugouts cleared, and the two teams made their way off the field. A small crowd hovered near the bleachers close to Caleb, his mom and sister — and Ricky. Several Wolves, including Eric and Travis, were hoping for a chance to talk to the Otters' new star player.

Ricky punched Caleb lightly on the shoulder. "You'll get 'em next time, dude," he said. Then Ricky turned to the Caleb's teammates and said, "Great game, guys. Tough loss, but hold your heads high."

As if Ricky's words of encouragement were an invitation to chat, the other Wolves players closed in like a pack of reporters. Ricky obliged, answering their rapid-fire questions with patience.

After a while, Caleb said, "Can we go home?"

"Of course, sweetie," his mom said. She didn't seem to be using her keen Mom-sense to know that Caleb was bummed out about the game.

Without saying goodbye to his teammates, Caleb walked away from the crowd and off toward his mom's car.

CHAPTER 3

AIN'T GOT THAT SWING

The image of Caleb's dad was brightly displayed on the small screen of Caleb's phone. He wore sunglasses and was walking around outside. "Your mom told me you lost yesterday," he said.

"Yep," Caleb replied. "Lost by one run." He didn't mention the fact that his embarrassing strikeout was how the game ended. He was pretty sure his mom had already told his dad to avoid the topic. His dad had probably called to make him feel better.

"Sorry to hear that," his dad said. Caleb could see a large construction site and a patch of palm trees behind his dad on the phone screen. It was a stark contrast to the dark basement where Caleb currently slouched on the couch. Nearby, soft music filtered out of the basement bedroom where Ricky was staying.

The last time Caleb went to visit his dad and Rebecca, they'd talked about a summer visit back to Minnesota. Caleb wanted to ask his dad about it now. But when Caleb opened his mouth to ask, his dad cut him off.

"No," Caleb's dad said. His face turned away. "The pallets should go over by the gazebo."

Clearly, he wasn't talking to Caleb. So Caleb just waited and watched his dad wander through the construction site.

Caleb waited a while. "Dad?" he finally asked.

His dad nearly jumped in shock. "Oh, sorry, pal," he said. "Aw man, I gotta go, Caleb."

"Okay."

"Tell your sister hi. I love —"

The image on the screen froze. Then the message *Poor Connection* appeared.

Caleb sighed and tossed his phone onto the couch beside him. "Figures," he muttered.

A moment later, Ricky poked his head out of the bedroom door. It was almost as if he were waiting for the right time. "Hey," he said. "Want to hit the batting cage?"

Caleb shrugged. "I'm no good at the plate. So why try?"

Ricky looked offended. "Come on, now," he said. "By *trying* is how you will *know*."

Ricky was right. Caleb *should* have been excited to practice. But he couldn't get the image of his distracted dad out of his head.

Hopefully, the batting cage would change that.

* * *

The batting cages were located in a drab cement building about a block from Gordon's Hardware Field. Ricky, dressed as colorfully as ever in a vibrant blue polo shirt and dashing red shorts, strolled in like he owned the place. A sleek black wooden bat was perched on one shoulder. Caleb followed closely behind, cradling his helmet and bat in his arms.

The cages were busy, filled with the constant pop and crack of machines and bats. Ricky found the only open cage, dropped a helmet on his head, and stepped inside.

"Watch and learn, amigo," he said to Caleb. "Watch and learn."

Ricky wiggled his bat and then used it to press the button on the mechanical box inside the batting cage. A moment later, the first pitch whizzed in at about 80 miles per hour.

Without hesitation, Ricky swung and connected. The ball struck the net at the far end of the cage.

Caleb, standing outside the cage with a helmet on, said, "Whoa. Yeah, I could never do that."

"Do not say that," Ricky said. Another ball exited the pitching machine with a *whoomp* sound. Ricky made contact with it while he spoke. "When I was a boy —" *Crack!* — "it was just my mother and me. I did not have a team in school, so I learned to pitch and hit from watching television and from practicing with my friends."

Caleb thought of Ricky growing up with just his mother. He realized that they might have more in common than he originally thought.

"As long as you keep at it," Ricky said, "you will gain the confidence and the ability to hit." Ricky smacked another of the pitches delivered by the machine. If they'd been at the ballpark, Caleb was sure the ball would have sailed over the fence.

"Now it is time for you to give it a try," Ricky said. He flipped the metal bat in his hand and offered the handle to Caleb.

"Okay," said Caleb.

The amount of confidence in Caleb's single word wouldn't have filled a thimble. He took the bat, adjusted his helmet, and stepped into the cage. He felt like he was a lion tamer being locked in with a vicious feline. The pitching machine stared down at him. He tensed, waiting for the first pitch.

"The key is to see the ball the moment it leaves the hand of the pitcher," Ricky explained. "It is hard to do here, but in a game, you will know. Each pitch has a different movement. Once you know what to expect, you will know how to swing."

The machine whirred, Caleb gripped his bat, and a ball came rocketing toward him.

Thwack!

It struck the backstop of the cage before Caleb could even get the bat around.

"Good start!" Ricky said.

"You must have been watching the kid in the next cage," Caleb muttered.

"Choke up on the handle," Ricky added quickly. "Time your swing."

The pitching machine fired, and Caleb took the advice. He still missed.

"I can't do it," Caleb said.

"You can," Ricky replied. "Be confident. Puff out your chest. Be the boss!" He laughed.

I'm sure glad one *of us is having a great time,* Caleb thought.

Another ball sailed in. Again, Caleb missed.

"This is dumb," Caleb said. He started to walk toward the cage gate.

Ricky whistled, and the sound cut through the batting cages, making everyone turn and look. Caleb stopped in his tracks.

The pitching machine sent a ball toward Caleb, who ducked out of the way. Ricky pointed to the painted-on lines of the batter's box.

Caleb stepped back into the batter's box. He bent his knees and set the bat on his shoulder.

"Eye on the ball, right out of the machine," Ricky said.

Caleb waited, and when he saw the ball start its motion out of the machine, he squeezed his hands around the bat and swung.

Crack! The bat vibrated in his hands. The sensation crawled up his arms, past his elbows. The ball glanced off the side of the cage and landed at the back, near the pitching machine.

"Por la maceta!" Ricky exclaimed. "Excellent!" He whistled again.

Caleb could feel his cheeks grow warm. His heart hammered in his chest. Sure, it had been one hit, and a weak one at that. But having someone like Ricky in his corner, cheering him on, made him want to step right back into the batter's box for another crack.

So he did.

CHAPTER 4

IN THE STANDS

"Boy-oh-boy! It's a beautiful afternoon for baseball!" The announcer's voice boomed from the sound system at Gordon's Hardware Field.

The sun was high in the sky, and a cool breeze cut across the field and bleachers. Caleb and his friend Eric stood near the home team dugout, trying to get as close to the action as they could.

"We've got a great game all set for you today between the Prairie Lake Otters and the Durston Ducks," the announcer continued. "So what do you say? Let's . . . *play ball!*"

Caleb and Eric joined the whoops and hollers from the crowd as the Otters jogged onto the field in their yellow and blue uniforms. "There's Ricky!" Eric shouted, nudging Caleb and pointing to the infield. Ricky strode out to his position at shortstop like he owned the whole diamond.

Caleb cupped his hands around his mouth and shouted, "Go, Alvarez!"

Ricky looked over, saw him, and pointed at the two boys. He flashed a wide grin.

"His first game as an Otter, and he doesn't look nervous at all," Eric marveled.

"I'd be terrified," Caleb said.

Ricky was right at home, though. When the second batter of the game hit a scorching ground ball to shortstop, Ricky swiped the ball with a flash of leather. Then he threw a perfect bullet across to the first baseman. The Duck batter was out before he'd made it halfway to first base.

"Wow!" said Eric. "That was impressive."

Otter fans thought the same thing, giving Ricky a rousing round of applause. Caleb couldn't have been sure, but he thought he saw Ricky give a quick bow to the fans. If he was playing for Coach Bullock, Ricky would be benched for sure, no matter how skillful the play was.

After a scoreless top half of the first, the Otters came up to bat. Ricky batted third in the lineup. Caleb and Eric pressed themselves up to the chain-link fence next to the dugout.

The first Otter batter popped out to shallow right field, and the second hit a blooping single. That brought Ricky to the plate.

When Otter players stepped to the plate, the PA announcer played a short piece of music. The players usually picked their own music. It was typically a rock-and-roll, hip-hop, or country song. But as Ricky strode up to the plate, the speakers played a fast-paced Latin song featuring trumpets, guitars, and maracas. Ricky looked as if he was dancing to the music as he tapped each cleat with his bat and readied himself.

Ricky bent his knees and waggled his bat. He now wore a pair of bright yellow batting gloves. They were so colorful that they looked like they radiated sunshine. His bat seemed to flow in one smooth movement — behind his head, then in front, then behind. Caleb watched intently. The Ducks pitcher went into his wind-up. The ball flew past Ricky and snapped into the catcher's mitt.

"Ball," the ump said.

Ricky was patient. His eyes never left the pitcher. As the at bat continued, Caleb started to bend his knees along with Ricky. He swayed from side to side like the walk-up music was still playing. He twirled an imaginary bat in his hands.

On the fourth pitch, Ricky saw something he liked. In a flash, he swung and connected with the ball. It soared high, heading toward the gap between left and center field.

"Go! Go!" Caleb shouted. The Ducks outfielders couldn't track it down, and the ball landed just shy of the warning track. Ricky rounded first and slid safely into second. The lead runner scored, and the Otters had a 1-0 lead.

Ricky leapt to his feet. He clapped and pumped a fist as the crowd cheered him on.

By the third inning, it was clear the Otters had the Ducks' number. "Let's grab something to drink," Eric suggested, and the two boys headed for the nearest concession stand.

After getting two large sodas, the boys walked around the stadium. They ran into the team mascot, Otto Otter. Otto was a giant otter in a blue and yellow baseball uniform. An oversized blue cap sat crooked atop his head. And they visited Caleb's mom and sister, who were seated in the bleachers.

"What a great game," his mom said. "Did you see Ricky's hit?"

"Yeah," Caleb said. "It was . . ."

He trailed off. His attention was drawn to a pair of older men seated right down by home plate. They both had polo shirts and baseball caps on. Both carried clipboards. As the Otter pitcher went into his wind-up, one of the men held up a machine that looked like a navy blue hair dryer.

Caleb nodded at the men. "Those are scouts," he said to Eric. "Like, major league scouts. They're using a radar gun to track the pitcher's speed and writing down notes about all the players."

He knew that scouts sometimes showed up at Otters games. Two seasons ago, the Otters' sidearm pitcher, Jackson Fry, had been discovered by a scout. He now pitched for the Atlanta Braves' AAA team. But Caleb had never seen a scout (let alone two!) at an Otters game before. It was new and exciting. *Then again*, he thought, watching Ricky turn a beautiful double play out on the field, *there's a lot about the team that's new and exciting.*

When the game was over, the Otters had won by a score of 7-1. Ricky had another double and a sacrifice bunt that he'd beaten out for a single. It was a stellar introduction to the fans for the newest Otter.

As the bleachers emptied, Caleb's focus remained on the two scouts. He'd glanced at them occasionally during the game. He noticed them whispering eagerly to one another after Ricky's sensational second double.

Caleb slowly made his way down to the bleachers with the rest of the Otter fans. He kept his eyes on the scouts. His stomach was twisted into anxious knots by their presence. But he wanted to get close to them to hear what they were discussing.

As he and Eric reached the bottom of the bleachers, Caleb slowed, pretending to be interested in his phone. He could almost hear the scouts talking . . .

"That Alvarez kid," one of the men said. "He really hit —"

"Caleb!" his mom shouted, startling him. "Stop wasting time. Let's go."

"One second," he replied.

"No," his mom shot back. "We have guests coming for dinner and have to get home pronto."

Caleb cursed under his breath. He cast a last glance at the scouts. They were still chatting, oblivious to the kid who had been trying to eavesdrop on them.

CHAPTER 5

DINNER AND A GAME

The kitchen looked like a tornado had blasted through it. Dishes and plates and silverware covered every spare inch of counter space. And the food hadn't even been served yet.

Caleb's mom stood in the middle of the mess and shook her head. "I don't know how you talked me into letting you cook," she said to Ricky with a laugh while sipping from a glass of red wine.

Ricky danced in the middle of the mess. Latin music played from a small radio by the fridge.

He placed the glass lid on a simmering dish of delicious-smelling food on the stove. Caleb watched from the dining room table, where a handful of Otter players sat playing cards.

"Trust me," Ricky said. "The mess will be worth it. This is my grandmother's recipe for *pollo guisado*. It is a traditional dish of braised chicken from *Republica Dominicana*."

"Well, it smells wonderful," Caleb's mom said. "I have to give you that."

"Agreed!" said Neal Horton, an Otter outfielder.

"My grandmother taught my mother to cook," Ricky continued. "And my mother taught me. We made this dish together every week, especially after special events. The game today was very special."

"First win of the season," said Carlos Torres, the Otter catcher.

The win *was* pretty special. Caleb had nearly told Ricky and the others about the scouts. But then he balked, deciding to keep the info to himself.

Before long the special chicken dish was taken off the stove. Ricky prepped each plate, adding a heap of chicken alongside beans and rice. Even Bethany, who mostly just ate macaroni and cheese and applesauce pouches, was willing to try the special food.

"Hats off at the table," Caleb's mom said as the plates were served to the crew of hungry ballplayers. The young men hung their caps on the backs of their chairs. Caleb did the same. Just sitting among them made him feel more grown up.

When they were ready to eat, Ricky stood. "Okay," he said. "First, a few words. When I was a boy, my grandmother taught me what she called 'The Four Fs.' These four things are what tie us all together. They are truly the most important things in a person's life." He listed them off on his fingers. "Family. Friends. Faith . . . and food!"

"Aw yeah!" Neal piped up, clinking his silverware together.

"This baseball team," Ricky said, "is my family, because family is not defined by blood. Mrs. Parker, Caleb, Bethany . . . *you* are my family also. Gracias."

"Thank you, Ricky," Caleb's mom said. "We're so blessed to have you all here."

They dug in, eating with gusto. Caleb couldn't stop shoveling the amazing chicken, beans, and rice into his mouth.

"You like it, right?" Ricky asked him jokingly, nudging Caleb with his elbow.

"Mmph-hmmph," a full-mouthed Caleb said.

As they finished eating, the doorbell rang. Caleb didn't think he'd be able to move after stuffing himself. But he somehow managed to get up and answer the door. Eric stood on the stoop, glove in hand. He tossed a ball into the air.

"Hey," Eric said. "Some of the team are hitting the school field to play a pick-up game before it gets dark. You in?"

"Well, I kind of . . ." He hadn't told Eric about the Otters coming over for dinner after the game. If he had, his whole team would have swarmed his house.

Still, Eric could tell something was up. He craned his neck to see around Caleb. "Hey, Ricky," he said. Ricky had snuck up behind Caleb while the two boys had been talking.

"*Hola*," Ricky said. "Are you going to play some ball, Caleb?"

Caleb shrugged. "I suppose —"

"Boys!" Ricky shouted back into the house. "Who wants to play a game against Caleb and his friends?"

A round of cheers came from inside.

Eric looked puzzled. "Wait, was that . . . ?"

"A house full of Otters?" said Caleb. He nodded with a smile.

The team helped clean up, thanked Caleb's mom, grabbed ballgloves, and joined Caleb and Eric.

There was a park about a block from Caleb's house with a playground, a gazebo, and a baseball field. As they approached, Caleb spied several of his friends waiting in the dirt infield. When they saw who was accompanying Caleb and Eric, they couldn't contain their excitement.

"Whoa! It's the Otters!" Travis shouted, prompting laughs from the older players.

"I feel like a rock star," said Arnie Reynolds, the Otters' left fielder.

The boys crowded around the newcomers, quickly choosing teams. Caleb naturally wound up on Ricky's squad, and they took the field first. Ricky wound up at his usual position, shortstop, while Caleb opted to play first base.

During the first time through the lineup, Eric hit a bouncing grounder to short. Ricky played it perfectly and fired across the field to Caleb. The ball snapped into Caleb's mitt and made his hand sting. He hung onto the ball, though.

After the play was over, he took his glove off and jokingly waved his hand around. "I think you broke it," he wailed to Ricky, making the whole group burst out in laughter.

"What do you mean?" Ricky shot back. "I lobbed that one at you."

When it was Caleb's turn to bat, he thought back to his time at the cage with Ricky. As he stepped into the batter's box, he swayed from side to side and waved his bat like Ricky.

"Uh-oh," Arnie said. "We've got some kind of mini-Alvarez on our hands!"

Ricky laughed. "He has good taste in heroes."

"No way Coach Bullock would let you get away with those moves during a game," Eric shouted from center field.

Caleb kept his eye on the ball, waiting until he found a pitch he liked. Swinging hard, he connected, sending a shot over the second baseman's head.

Ricky, waiting in the on-deck circle, raced down to first and gave Caleb a huge high-five. "That is how you do it!" he shouted.

Caleb laughed. He looked to the field's backstop and saw his mom and Bethany behind it. Ricky noticed as well. He jogged over and talked Caleb's mom into letting Bethany join them as umpire.

When Travis swung and missed for strike three, Caleb's little sister shouted, "Youuuu're out!" at the top of her tiny lungs.

They played until the haze of night made it hard to see the ball. It was the most amazing, surreal experience of Caleb's life. As they walked back home, with the stars blinking on above them and the streetlights sparking through the neighborhood, Ricky slipped an arm around Caleb's shoulder.

"Great game, amigo," Ricky said.

No, Caleb thought, *not great. The best!*

CHAPTER 6

STANDING OUT

The Otters had their first away-from-home
series the following week. Caleb and his mom
dropped Ricky off at the team bus, and the
Otters drove north for a three-game stint against
the Horton Elks.

It was weird having the house to themselves
again. After only a couple of weeks of having
Ricky live in their basement, Caleb had grown
used to the constant noise and activity. He
missed it.

Each night, though, Caleb's phone would buzz. It was Ricky, checking in through text or video messaging. They chatted about the Otters game or Wolves game or even stuff as goofy as the hotel room service at the Horton Inn.

While Ricky was away, Caleb kept working hard at the plate. The Wolves picked up their first win, thanks to a late home run by Anthony Carbini and great pitching by Omar Nabeen. After striking out during his first at bat, Caleb found the outfield during his second time at the plate. He blooped a single over the third baseman's head. Of course, the Wolves were already up 5-0, so there was no pressure. Still, it felt great to read the ball out of the pitcher's hand and know when to swing at it.

When Caleb got home that evening, he shot Ricky an excited text: *WE WON! & I GOT A HIT!*

Ricky immediately wrote back: *KNEW U COULD DO IT!*

The Wolves' next game was in two days.

By then, the Otters would be back from Horton and Ricky would be in attendance. Unlike the last time Caleb's new friend was at a Wolves game, *this* time he couldn't wait for Ricky to see him play.

It wasn't until the following morning at breakfast that Caleb realized he had forgotten to video chat with his dad after the game. When he tried to call his dad, he received no answer.

Ten minutes later, his dad sent a text: *SORRY PAL. ON SITE. WILL CALL YOU IN AN HOUR.*

But he didn't.

* * *

"Stay focused out there," Coach Bullock said in his abrupt voice. "Let's build on our last win and keep momentum on —"

"Let's go, Wolves!" Ricky's said, walking behind the dugout's chain-link fence. "Have some fun out there!"

Coach Bullock frowned.

Caleb knew he didn't like being interrupted. He could see the man was fuming inside.

Ricky must have noticed it, as well. "Sorry, Coach," he said. "I did not mean to put my voice on the top of yours."

"Wolves," Coach Bullock said through gritted teeth, "take the field."

Caleb started the game in right field, which he didn't mind. There usually wasn't too much action there, which meant less chance of botching a fly ball. Omar mowed down the Hornets in order, striking out the side and bringing the home team to the plate.

Caleb was batting seventh, behind the power hitters. When the Wolves started the second inning with a pair of singles, Caleb came up to the plate.

"You got this!" Ricky cheered from the bleachers. Caleb dug in to the batter's box and waited for the first pitch.

Caleb's batting average, especially with runners in scoring position, was low. It was the pressure again. It messed with his confidence, and the next thing he knew . . .

"Strike one!"

He hadn't been paying attention. He glanced at the third base coach, Anthony Carbini's dad. He was flashing signs like he was being attacked by a swarm of bugs. In all that mess of signals, Caleb caught a belt buckle brush followed by an ear tug.

Bunt.

Clearly, Coach Bullock wanted a straightforward sacrifice bunt to move the runners up a base. As the pitcher delivered, Caleb squared up and placed the bat across the plate.

The pitch was a curveball. Caleb stabbed at it. The ball popped up into the air.

"Mine!" the pitcher called out, waving everyone off and easily catching it for an out.

Dejected, Caleb walked back to the dugout.

Ricky was waiting for him by the fence. "Hold your head up," Ricky said. "You will get it next time. Be courageous and take chances."

Coach Bullock, who was also the team's first base coach, glared at Ricky but said nothing.

The botched play was an omen of things to come. Neither team could get any offense going. Whenever someone *did* get on base, the following batters couldn't get them across. It was like the two teams were just going through the motions, which resulted in an excruciating 0-0 game after five innings.

But when the Wolves came up to bat in the sixth inning, the whole game changed. Eric drew a walk from the solid Hornet pitcher. Then he made it to second base after Anthony flied out to left field.

That brought Caleb up to bat.

As he started to walk from the on-deck circle, a sound began to fill the air.

It took Caleb a second to figure out what it was: Latin music. In fact, it was Ricky's walk-up music. It was the same song they played every time he came to the plate at Gordon Field.

Caleb looked out at the stands. Ricky held his phone, turned up to full volume, up over his head. "Come on, little man!" he shouted. Then he let out one of his patented Ricky whistles.

Caleb's mood lightened. He felt like a load had been lifted from his shoulders and walked in rhythm up to the plate.

Ricky stopped the music then, but Caleb could still feel it buzzing in his chest. He bent his knees and waggled his bat back and forth like Ricky did. The bat moved forward, back, forward, back.

Caleb watched the ball come out of the pitcher's hand perfectly. He saw it streaking straight down the heart of the plate and . . .

Crack!

He hit a liner over the pitcher's head, past the diving second baseman, and out into right-center.

"Excelenté!" Ricky shouted.

Caleb watched as Eric scampered toward third base. The throw came in behind him, and he easily beat it out.

Runners at first and third, with one out. Caleb looked over to third and saw Anthony's dad giving the signs. Nothing. Caleb danced off first, getting a solid lead. Travis was up to bat now. The pitcher went into the wind-up, and Travis hit a weak grounder toward third base.

Caleb took off for second, but he couldn't help watching the play unfold. Eric broke for home, even though the ball was just 20 feet from the plate.

What is he doing?! thought Caleb. *There's no way he'll make it in time.*

The pitcher ran forward to grab it, diving and flipping the ball to the catcher.

There was an explosion of dust. From it, the umpire emerged. He spread his arms out like a bird's and cried, "Safe!"

Eric jumped to his feet and pointed out to the bleachers. He did a little dance move. "That's what I'm talking about!" Ricky shouted over the sound of the cheering fans.

Caleb and Travis remained stranded on-base for the rest of the inning. But the Wolves managed to finish off the Hornets in the top of the seventh. Caleb even caught the last out, a shallow fly ball to right field.

After the game, Coach Bullock gathered the team in the outfield. "Take a knee," he said. Caleb did as he was instructed. Most boys knelt, while a few others sat in the grass.

"That was a decent performance today," Coach Bullock said. "However, you'll all need to play a solid game next week when we take on the Bradbury Stallions. They're undefeated."

"Yeah? We'll change that," Travis said, slapping his fist into his mitt with a *thunk* sound.

"Pipe down," Coach Bullock said. "Don't get overconfident. Be prepared and be smart. Listen to your coaches. We know what's best for the team. Now go home and rest up."

"Home?" a voice chimed in.

Caleb didn't even have to turn around to know who had spoken up. Ricky's accent and chipper tone was unmistakable. "Who can go home after such a great win? These boys deserve some ice cream cones!"

The team cheered and leapt to their feet.

Coach Bullock said nothing. But he didn't have to . . . his scowl said it all.

CHAPTER 7

GOOD NEWS/BAD NEWS

The best ice cream in Prairie Lake was sold at a small outdoor place called Towering Cones. The small shop was located right off the lake, near a public beach and boat launch. A neon ice cream cone gleamed above the walk-up window. Plenty of picnic tables provided the perfect spot to sit after a long day. Caleb and his dad used to be frequent customers, often after taking the boat out on Prairie Lake, where they'd fish for hours and wind up hitting their limit of crappies and sunfish.

Now, though, Caleb wasn't thinking of his dad. He was sitting at one of the picnic tables with his teammates.

"I saw that grounder and thought, *I gotta score!*" Eric recalled the game-winning run. He mimicked his dash down the base path and dropped a scoop of his ice cream to the ground.

"Ha! Nice one!" Travis barked, laughing at his friend. Caleb joined in as Eric stared down at his ruined treat.

Caleb took a lick of his pistachio ice cream. Ricky had convinced him to try it. Despite Caleb's doubts, he had to admit that it tasted delicious.

"Hey, Caleb," Anthony said. "What was with that funky music during the game?"

Caleb shrugged. "Ask Ricky," he replied.

"I've used that song, "*Diviertete,*" as walk-up music my whole baseball career," Ricky explained. "It is a song that means 'Enjoy Yourself!' Because that's what baseball should be . . . a joy!"

"Not the way Coach Bullock plays it," Eric grumbled. Some of the other players agreed. Coach Bullock, not surprisingly, had passed on the chance to join them for ice cream.

"Baseball is supposed to be fun," Ricky said. "Maybe your coach just needs you to show him how fun it can be."

Ricky was right. Baseball was supposed to be enjoyable. Maybe that was why Caleb had so much trouble batting in clutch situations — he had forgotten he was playing a fun sport with his friends. If he just let himself enjoy the moment, then maybe his confidence would go up.

"Ricky," Eric asked, taking a huge bite of his Rocky Road cone, "what's the funniest thing that's happened to you playing baseball?"

"Oh wow." Ricky thought for a moment. "Where to start? The time my friend put glue on my batting gloves right before I was up to bat? Or when I blew a gigantic bubble gum bubble and stuck it to my coach's cap? Or maybe the time a cow wandered onto our field as I was chasing after a fly ball?"

"Yeah! Tell us more about that one!" Eric asked.

Ricky laughed and began to tell the story. "It was a baseball field surrounded by farms, back in the Dominican. Very small field, small crowd. A herd of cows was grazing nearby. I was playing left field, and the fence —" he raised a hand to about chest-level, "— was this high, not very sturdy. One cow, he gets through the fence and onto the field. I don't see him, and this player, he hits a monster of a fly ball."

Ricky began to perform the action as he spoke, pretending he had a mitt on his hand. He looked up at the sky. "I lost it in the sun for a moment but never stopped running backward. *Keep your eyes on the ball* . . . that's what your coaches say, right? So I did. So I didn't know the cow was there until —"

Here, he stopped.

The boys, spellbound, waited for Ricky to continue. Instead, he held up one finger. "One moment." He dug his phone out of his pocket, and Caleb saw it was buzzing. Ricky's eyes lit up. He quickly hurried away from the boys.

"He totally ran into that cow, didn't he?" Eric suggested.

"Well, it's not like the thing could moooo-ve out of his way!" Travis added.

The Wolves groaned at this bad joke, and several threw their balled-up napkins at him.

Caleb wasn't paying attention to the boys, though. He had his eyes on Ricky, who was pacing back and forth by the Towering Cones building. He listened, spoke briefly, and listened again. Caleb even saw him chewing his fingernails, something he'd never seen Ricky do before.

Something's up, Caleb thought. Suddenly, the cold pit in his stomach wasn't because of the pistachio ice cream.

Ricky remained on the phone for several more painfully long minutes. Caleb was so intrigued by Ricky's conversation that his ice cream cone dripped down over his fingers. Finally, Ricky hung up the phone and gave a fist pump.

Caleb watched him walk back over to the boys. But something was *different*. His steps were lighter, his smile wider.

"Who was that?" Caleb said. He wanted to play it cool, to see if Ricky would share whatever good news he'd just gotten on his own. But the words slipped from Caleb's mouth before he could stop them.

Ricky shrugged. "No one important," he said. Then, after a long pause, he added, "Just a scout for the Kansas City Royals!"

Ricky leapt into the air. The Wolves did the same as Ricky's excitement caught them up like a frenzied twister. "They want me to fly down to try out for their AA minor-league team!"

"That's great!" Eric said.

"Way to go!" Anthony cried.

Caleb, however, was silent.

A try out for an actual Major League Baseball team? That was a big deal. Ricky had talent. The scouts at the Otters game had seen it. And the more Caleb thought about it, he was pretty sure that one had been wearing a polo shirt with the Royals' KC logo on it.

But if Ricky made the team, that would mean an end to his time in Prairie Lake with the Otters. And an end to his time with Caleb.

"Caleb?" Eric was trying to get his attention, but Caleb had been lost in thought.

"Huh?" said Caleb.

"I said . . . *isn't that amazing?*" said Eric. "Ricky is gonna try out for the Royals!"

"Yeah," Caleb said. "Totally."

But when he looked at Ricky, he could tell his new friend had come to the same realization.

Ricky knew exactly why Caleb wasn't as ecstatic as the others.

"So when's the big day?" Anthony asked.

"Next Tuesday," Ricky said. "But they want me there on Monday."

"Hey, that's the day of our game against the Bradbury Stallions," Travis said.

"Too bad you'll miss it," Eric said. "You'll be miles away from us!"

"Yeah," Caleb said, dropping the rest of his pistachio ice cream cone in the trash. "Too bad."

CHAPTER 8

IT'S SO HARD TO SAY GOODBYE

When Caleb's mom came by to pick them up from Towering Cones, he climbed silently into the car. It took Ricky one block to share his news. Caleb's mom was floored and excited. Caleb wished he felt that way. He really did. He wanted to be happy for his new friend. But he'd already been abandoned by one important person in his life. Now he had the chance of losing another.

He knew it was stupid, but it didn't change how he felt.

Ricky talked the entire drive home. He discussed his plane ride, and how he needed to call his coach, and how the other guys would feel about his big shot. More than once, Caleb caught his mom's eyes looking at him in the rearview mirror.

Once home, Caleb went right to his room to change out of his uniform. But he also wanted space and silence.

He had it for about three minutes. Then there was a soft rapping on his door.

"Come in," he said flatly.

The door opened a bit, and his mom's head poked in. "Got a second?" she asked.

He'd half-expected his visitor was going to be Ricky. He figured chatting with his mom instead was probably for the best just then. He opened the door further but continued to not speak.

"Mind if I sit?" she said, indicating the messy bed.

Caleb nodded.

After a moment of uncomfortable silence, his mom said, "Cool news about Ricky, huh?"

Caleb shrugged. "I'm pretty tired," he said. "So I think I'm just gonna get some pajamas on and call it a night."

"At seven o'clock? On a summer night?" His mom placed the back of her hand on his forehead. "Are you all right?"

Caleb brushed his mom's hand away.

She didn't stand up to leave, though. "You know," she said. "Bethany and I will still be in the stands cheering for you. We always are."

"Whatever. You're my mom," Caleb fired back. "You *have* to be there."

That wasn't fair. Caleb could see the hurt in his mom's eyes as she stood up. She was his rock, the only thing he could trust after his dad had left.

"I'll blame that one on you having brain freeze from all that ice cream," his mom said. "But you don't get another."

Caleb hung his head. "Sorry," he whispered.

His mom closed the door after her, leaving Caleb alone. Again.

* * *

"Come on, come on. Pick up."

It was the day of the game against the Bradbury Stallions. Caleb and his mom were about to take Ricky to Gordon Field, where the Otters had a car waiting to drive him to the airport. Caleb stared at his phone and the photo of his dad that popped up when he was trying to call him. He wanted to hear his dad's voice, to see him for just a moment. But it wasn't looking like either of those things were going to happen. Typical.

"Let's go, Caleb!" his mom called from the door. "Bring your bag! We're going straight to the game!"

Caleb ended the call without leaving a message. Then he grabbed his baseball bag off his bed and raced down to join the others.

Caleb was in full uniform, aside from the pair of sneakers on his feet. He threw his bag into the trunk next to Ricky's bright red duffel bag and slammed it closed. Then he slid into the backseat beside Bethany in her booster.

The days since Ricky's big announcement had gone by in a blur. Ricky had spent much of his time at the ball field, preparing for his tryout. Caleb had spoken to him very little. Some of that wasn't on purpose, because of their busy schedules. But some of it . . . was. He still felt hurt that Ricky may be leaving them, right when Caleb was getting used to having the ballplayer around.

"So you have your flight information, Ricky?" Caleb's mom asked as they pulled into the baseball field's parking lot.

A black car was parked across two spots, its driver leaning against it.

Ricky held up the boarding pass they'd printed at home. "Yes, ma'am," he said.

Caleb's mom pulled up beside the other car, and they got out. The car's driver immediately went to the trunk and removed Ricky's duffel bag.

"We'll see you in a couple of days, right?" Caleb's mom asked.

"Absolutely," he answered.

"I'll miss you!" Bethany said. She wrapped her arms around Ricky's legs.

"You take care of your big brother for me," Ricky said. "Cheer him on today."

Caleb stood back and waited until they were finished. Then Ricky held out a hand. "Good luck, my man," he said. "You will call me when the game is over?"

"Sure," Caleb said.

"Do not be so glum," Ricky smiled. "I will be back soon. It's just a tryout."

Caleb knew better, though. Ricky was one of the best baseball players he'd ever met. There was no way the Royals wouldn't snatch him up.

Then Ricky would be gone. *So much for The Four Fs,* Caleb thought.

"I have something for you," Ricky said. He reached into his back pocket and pulled out a pair of bright yellow batting gloves. They were identical to the ones Ricky wore. He held them out to Caleb. "Wear them today," he said.

Caleb took the gloves. "Thanks," he said quietly, knowing full well that he wouldn't wear the gloves.

Then, before Caleb could protest, Ricky drew him in for a quick hug.

"Remember, Caleb," Ricky said. "It is a beautiful day for baseball. So enjoy yourself!"

Then Ricky slid into the backseat of the black car. The driver closed the door after him.

Caleb and his family stood together and watched as the car drove out of the lot and off toward the airport.

CHAPTER 9

HEAD IN THE GAME

Ricky had been right; it *was* a beautiful day for baseball. The sun was out, and there wasn't a cloud in the sky. But Caleb didn't really feel like playing. He wanted to go home, play video games, and try to forget about the rest of the world for a while.

Of course, that wasn't an option.

By the time they made it to the field, the other Wolves players were already there. Caleb sulked over to the dugout and plopped down on a bench.

He rooted around in his bag for his cleats while some of the other players huddled around him. He shoved the yellow batting gloves into his back pocket.

"So did Ricky leave for his tryout or what?" Travis asked.

"He must be almost to the airport by now, right?" Eric said.

Anthony smacked a fist into his mitt. "He's gonna be a major-leaguer someday. I just know it."

Caleb laced up his cleats, wishing he could go back to being the guy that no one paid much attention to.

"I hope you gentlemen are discussing the game," Coach Bullock said as he strode over to the pack of Wolves. "Otherwise get onto the field for warm-ups."

For once, Caleb was thankful for Coach Bullock's attitude. It relieved him of answering any more questions about Ricky.

He grabbed his glove and jogged onto the field to play catch with Eric, who was waiting for him.

Caleb glanced at the opposing team. The Stallions were intimidating. They all looked tall and lean, especially their pitcher, who was warming up along the third base line. Each pitch popped loudly into the catcher's mitt.

Soon, it was time for the home team Wolves to take the field. Caleb made his way out to right field. The umpire shouted, "Play ball!"

The Stallions wasted no time. On the very first pitch of the game, the lead-off hitter smacked a long fly ball to the gap in left-center. It struck the fence before either of the Wolves in the area could catch it. He slid in for a triple.

Oh man, Caleb thought. *It's going to be one of those games.*

The next batter hit a single up the middle, scoring the player on third. After two pitches, the Wolves were down 1-0.

As the third Stallion stepped up to the plate, Caleb's mind began to drift. He thought about Ricky climbing into the car at Gordon Field and of the car driving off. It wasn't like he thought Ricky was going to live with them forever. Hosting an Otter was just for the season after all. But it had only been a couple of weeks, and Caleb had bonded with Ricky more than anyone.

More than he had with anyone since his dad —

Crack!

"Caleb!" Coach Bullock shouted out. "That's your ball!"

The Stallion batter had slugged a high fly ball. Caleb had missed it coming off the bat, and quickly scanned the brilliant blue sky for the ball.

Where is it? Where is it?

At the last second, he spied the ball sailing toward him. It had already begun to fall as Caleb rushed forward. He wasn't going to make it to the ball in time.

His best move would be to pull up, glove it on the bounce, and throw it in. It would go for a single. But Caleb couldn't accept that.

Just before the ball was about to hit the ground, Caleb launched himself into the air. He stretched his glove out in front of him. He was parallel to the ground, diving toward the fly ball . . .

But he missed it by a foot. Caleb hit the ground like he was belly-flopping into a swimming pool. The air rushed from his lungs. He was too dazed to even move. The ball bounced past him and rolled to the fence. The centerfielder raced after it as Caleb rolled over to watch. The Stallions fans whooped and hollered.

By the time the ball had reached the cut-off man, the batter was standing on third.

Caleb pushed himself to his knees, tried to take a deep breath, and coughed. Pinpricks of pain spread across his chest. He stood and wiped the grass from his uniform.

Coach Bullock just stared at him. He didn't even ask if Caleb was all right.

After another single drove home the runner on third, the Wolves were able to get a strikeout and two grounders. The score was 3-0, and they hadn't even batted yet.

As Caleb jogged to the dugout, Coach Bullock stopped him. "That was a routine single," he said. "Don't be a hero. Just play the game, and be smart about it."

"Yes, sir," Caleb said quietly.

The Stallions' first inning runs changed the mood in the Wolves dugout. The team was grim and brooding, and the Stallions pitcher quickly struck out their side. Before Caleb knew it, he was headed back onto the field.

When it was Caleb's turn to bat in the next inning, he trudged up to the batter's box.

Caleb stared at the pitcher, whose cap was pulled low to hide his eyes.

The Stallion hurler went into his wind-up and released the pitch . . .

"Strike one!" the ump called. Caleb couldn't believe it. He'd barely seen the ball leave the pitcher's hand.

You can do this, he told himself. Caleb tried to feel the music in his chest again, but without Ricky to cheer him on, it was gone.

The pitcher shook off the first sign, and then nodded at the next. When the second pitch came at him, Caleb squeezed his eyes shut and swung.

"Strike two!"

Caleb gripped his bat hard. He could feel the frustration burbling up like lava through cracked earth. He squinted down at the pitcher. The Stallion went into his wind-up and fired the ball.

Caleb swung with all his might. However, the pitch was a change-up. It dropped into the catcher's mitt easily.

"Strike three!" the ump cried. "You're out!"

Caleb spun on a heel and stalked back to the dugout. "You'll get it next time, bud!" his mom shouted from the bleachers.

Like a cracked dam finally breaking from the pressure, Caleb's pent-up anger got the best of him. As he reached the dugout, he pulled off his helmet and chucked it hard against the fence.

"Whoa!" Eric shouted.

"I can't do this!" Caleb said through gritted teeth. He slammed his bat against the wooden bench, turned around —

And saw Coach Bullock glaring at him again.

"I don't know what your deal is, Parker," Coach Bullock said. "But if I see one more outburst, just one, you're benched for the rest of the game." He paused and then added, "Maybe the season."

Caleb sat down heavily on the bench. None of the others players talked to him.

Keeping pace with the hard-hitting Stallions was a difficult task for the Wolves.

Two innings and two more runs later, the score was 5-0.

The Wolves didn't have many more chances. And Caleb was back in the on-deck circle.

As he lazily practiced swinging, he came up with the same plan he had during the first game of the season: *Don't swing*. At all. The Stallions pitcher was still firing strikes. He'd be back on the bench in three pitches.

Ahead of him, Eric cracked a two-out single to left field, giving the Wolves their first baserunner of the game.

"Come on, Caleb!" his sister's tiny voice shouted. She seemed to be the only one with any faith left in the team.

Caleb took one last practice swing, adjusted his helmet, and began to walk up to the batter's box.

And that was when Caleb heard a very distinctive whistle.

CHAPTER 10

COMEBACK

Caleb stopped in his tracks.

"Ricky?"

He peered at the bleachers. *I must be hearing things,* he thought. *Ricky's at the airport. He's probably just now boarding his plane and heading off to his tryout.*

Then he heard the whistle again and looked toward the dugout. His mom was standing there, which struck Caleb as weird. She always sat in the bleachers.

Ricky wasn't with her. But she *was* holding up her phone.

Caleb glanced over to first base, where Coach Bullock stood like a stone-faced soldier. *One more outburst*, he'd said. *Just one.* What he was about to do could get him benched for the season. He knew that.

He did it anyway.

Caleb hurried back to the dugout so fast that he nearly ran into the chain-link fence by his mom. Ricky's face was plastered on the phone screen, smiling out at him.

"Hey, little man!" Ricky said. Caleb could see large windows behind Ricky. A plane was lifting off into the sky.

"Ricky!" Caleb said. "What are you doing?"

"I am trying to watch my favorite team play their most important game of the season," Ricky replied. "My flight was delayed, so I gave your mom a call right away."

Caleb felt a renewed strength and vigor wash over him. "We're getting our butts kicked," he said.

"So change that, man! Enjoy yourself out there! Keep your eye on the ball!"

Other Wolves had crowded around Caleb. It seemed like the whole team had received new life.

"What's going on over there?!" the ump shouted. "Batter up!"

"I gotta go," Caleb said.

"Yeah, you do." Ricky laughed. "Go and hit a home run."

Caleb's mom held the phone up high so Ricky could watch. Caleb looked down at Coach Bullock. His face remained the same, but he said nothing to Caleb. As Caleb walked to the plate, his teammates began to chant something from the dugout. At first he couldn't make it out, because they weren't saying words. Rather, they were . . . singing?

Then it hit him. The whole team was singing the song *"Diviertete."*

Caleb stopped. He reached into his pocket and pulled out the yellow gloves Ricky had given him.

He slipped them on, then stepped into the batter's box with extra swagger. He moved his hips back and forth and swayed his bat from front to back, front to back.

The pitcher must not have expected Caleb to swing. He wound up and delivered a fastball right down the middle of the plate.

Caleb saw it leave his hand. Without a second thought, he swung.

Crack!

The ball launched off his bat like it had been fired from a cannon. It sailed high into the air, out toward right-center field. Caleb dropped his bat and bolted toward first.

Ricky's signature whistle cut through the cheers.

The right fielder had a shot at the ball and dove to catch it. He missed, though, and the ball shot past his glove.

"Go! Go!" Coach Bullock shouted, waving his arms frantically.

Caleb rounded first and headed for second. Ahead of him, Eric was already cruising past third and was on his way home.

As he reached second, Caleb looked toward Anthony's dad coaching at third. He was still waving his arms, signaling Caleb to keep running. He did, his legs pumping furiously. Behind him, Caleb could hear the Stallions calling for the cut-off man to catch the ball.

Caleb didn't slow down. He barreled toward home. He could sense the ball was coming in. The catcher was crouching, waiting for the relay throw.

Caleb slid headfirst as the ball hit the catcher's mitt with a *thwack* sound. He stretched forward as the catcher squatted down to apply the tag. Caleb's fingers brushed the plate . . .

"Safe!" the ump bellowed.

Caleb leaped to his feet. He brushed dirt from his chest as the team swarmed the plate to give him high-fives.

"An inside-the-park home run!" Eric shouted. "That was amazing!"

Caleb beamed with pride as the team headed back to the dugout. The score was now 5-2, and they were still losing. But Caleb's at-bat had sparked them back to life.

The following inning, the Wolves rally continued. Anthony hit a solo home run. Then two more batters came through with a pair of perfect back-to-back singles to cut the Stallions lead to 5-4. The flustered Stallions pitcher was taken out of the game, replaced by a reliever who didn't have the same arm strength.

Heading into the bottom of the seventh, and their last chance to bat, the Wolves still needed one run to tie and two to win.

Travis led off, hitting a ground ball that bounced high and gave the shortstop trouble. He made it to first easily. Anthony followed by hitting a liner over third base that was just fair.

"We've got this, Wolves!" Eric shouted.

But then the next batter popped out to first.

One out.

Eric was next up to bat.

The runners were still at first and second. On the second pitch, Eric sent a fly ball to deep right. The Stallions outfielder caught it, but the runners were able to tag up and each advance a base.

Two outs.

Once again, Caleb was up to bat.

As he strolled up to the plate, Caleb looked down the third base line at Mr. Carbini. As he did, Coach Bullock shouted, "Parker!" Caleb shifted his attention to first base instead. Coach Bullock was giving him the signs this time, pawing at his chest and hat like he'd lost his keys or something. But Caleb caught the sign hidden in the middle of it.

Bunt?

He must have missed it. A bunt with two outs? That was unheard of!

A smirking Coach Bullock gave the signs again, and sure enough, there it was.

He wants me to bunt.

Caleb thought back to the last time he'd tried bunting, and how he'd popped out to the pitcher. If he did that again, the game was over.

But you are not going to do that again, Caleb heard Ricky's voice in his head. *You are going to surprise them all!*

Caleb stepped into the box. He waved his bat around, looking like he was ready to hit another inside-the-park home run. The Stallion infield backed up several steps.

Caleb felt the pressure start to close in on him. He hated these situations. But the situation was here, and the time to act was now.

He was confident he could hit the ball.

The pitcher went into the wind-up.

Caleb waited.

The pitcher's arm came forward.

Caleb waited.

The pitcher released the ball.

And Caleb squared up to bunt.

He caught the whole Stallion team off-guard. The third baseman looked like he'd been struck by lightning. He jolted up. Travis, leading off third base, broke for home. He and the third baseman ran side by side as the ball hurtled toward Caleb.

Caleb pushed the bat forward, striking the ball perfectly. The bunt dropped to the ground, rolling up the first base line.

Pushing his legs harder than he ever had before, Caleb dashed for first base. He heard Travis slide safely into home. Now he just had to beat the throw to first.

Seconds became hours. Split seconds became eons. Each step felt like a mile.

You can make it, Caleb repeated to himself. He was almost there. In front of him, the first baseman tensed to catch the ball.

Just as Caleb touched first base, the ball went sailing over the baseman's head. The pitcher, who had fielded the ball, had overthrown first base!

Anthony hurried around third, heading for home. The Wolves dugout was jumping up and down. Caleb turned around to watch, and saw his teammate cross home plate without even sliding.

We won!

They'd beaten the undefeated Stallions!

* * *

Caleb adjusted the left side of the banner hanging in his living room and secured it with tape. The sign read, in bold and colorful letters, *Congratulations, Ricky!* Around him, the house was filled with life. People. Music. Food. It was overwhelming, but in the best way imaginable.

It had been almost a week since Ricky's tryout and the Wolves' come-from-behind victory against the Stallions. Caleb's team was still riding high.

The guys were ready to take on any challenge. Coach Bullock was still as strict as ever. But when Eric had used his bat as a microphone to sing during batting practice, Caleb could have sworn he'd seen Coach crack a smile.

Caleb looked around the room. Many of the Otters players had joined them to celebrate Ricky's exciting news. He and the Royals had agreed to a minor-league contract. Ricky would be leaving to join the team in a week. Also at the party were many of Caleb's teammates.

A distinctive whistle cut through the air, and all conversation stopped. Ricky and Caleb's mom stood together near the table. It was heaped with food, including many authentic Dominican dishes Ricky had prepared.

"Thank you all for coming today!" Ricky said. "And thank you to Mrs. Parker and her family. I am truly humbled by this whole experience. Thank you all for your generosity and support."

Ricky had only lived with the Parkers for about a month, but Caleb had learned so much from him in that short period of time. And for that, he'd be forever grateful.

"As a boy, I learned right away how very special baseball was to me," Ricky continued. "How every time I walk onto that field, it will be a unique experience."

"You mean like the time you ran into that cow?" Eric hollered from the back of the crowd, drawing laughs.

Ricky chuckled and said, "That *cow* ran into *me.*" He saw Caleb in the crowd. "So my advice to you all would be this: Do not ever lose that feeling. *Diviertete.*"

The gathered crowd clapped.

Ricky finished by saying, "I cannot wait to share the next chapter with you all. Now . . . let us eat!"

ABOUT the AUTHOR

Brandon Terrell is the author of numerous children's books, including several volumes in both the *Tony Hawk 900 Revolution* series and the *Tony Hawk Live2Skate* series. He has also written several *Spine Shivers* titles and is the author of the *Sports Illustrated Kids: Time Machine Magazine* series. When not hunched over his laptop, Brandon enjoys watching movies and television, reading, watching and playing baseball, and spending time with his wife and two children at his home in Minnesota.

GLOSSARY

backstop (BAK-stop) — a fence, screen, or wall that is placed behind the catcher to prevent the ball from rolling away

batter's box (BAT-uhrs BOHKS) — rectangular area on either side of home plate where the batter stands when trying to hit a pitch

bunt (BUHNT) — to softly hit a pitch without taking a full swing in order to make it difficult to field

distinctive (dih-STINGK-tiv) — a unique quality or characteristic of something or someone

intimidating (in-TIM-uh-dayt-ing) — describing someone or something that causes fear

on-deck circle (ON-DEK SUR-kuhl) — place where player next in line to bat warms up, often in a marked circle

reliever (ree-LEE-ver) — short for "relief pitcher," a pitcher who enters the game after the starting pitcher is removed

sacrifice (SAK-ruh-fise) — a batter's act of hitting a ball with the intention of advancing a baserunner

walk-up music (WAWK-up MYEW-zik) — musical piece or song played for a batter who is approaching home plate

DISCUSSION QUESTIONS

1. Ricky Alvarez lived in the Dominican Republic and moved to the United States. What are some cultural differences he may experience living in the U.S.?

2. Baseball is an important part of life to the people in Prairie Lake. Why? Are there examples in the story?

3. Coach Bullock and Ricky have different approaches to baseball. Which one do you agree with more?

WRITING PROMPTS

1. Pretend you are Caleb, and have just found out that Ricky Alvarez will be living with you. Write an email or postcard introducing yourself and your family to Ricky.

2. Ricky cooks traditional Dominican Republic food for Caleb and his family and friends. Write about a memorable meal you had that included new food you'd never tried before.

3. You are a school reporter watching the baseball game between the Wolves and the Stallions. Write an article describing the highlights of the game.

MORE ABOUT BASEBALL

Major League Baseball (MLB) players come from all over the world. As of the 2017 season opener, 230 players on MLB rosters were born outside of the United States. At least 17 different countries were represented, including Cuba, Venezuela, and Japan.

In 2017 the Dominican Republic had the most major league players from outside the U.S., with a total of 83.

In 2017 the MLB team with the most players from other countries was the Texas Rangers (15).

THE FUN DOESN'T STOP HERE!

FIND MORE AT:
CAPSTONEKIDS.COM

Authors and Illustrators | Videos and Contests
Games and Puzzles | Heroes and Villains

Find cool websites and
more books like this one at
www.facthound.com

Just type in the Book ID:
9781496559319
and you're ready to go!